A step in the direction of

Zen and the Art of Magenite Suspension

by Mighty Rahiem

ISBN-13: 978-0-9998398-2-9

Cover and illustrations by Mighty Rahiem

Dedicated to you, you fellow travellers
and dreamers and lovers of the journey;
I raise a bloody pith-helmet in your
honor.

As long as there is a story, you will
not be forgotten.

A note from the author

From the beginning, music has played an integral roll in Zerth's development. For this reason, you will find the names of songs and their respective artists in bold as they appear throughout the story. I would encourage you to indulge in the mood as you read. It's a gimmick, admittedly, but not intentionally so. I would argue that none of these stories would exist without them, so how could I leave them out? Soup without crackers? Preposterous. Coffee without cigarettes? Unthinkable. Zerth without music? You get the idea. So, I invite you to throw some soup on, pour yourself a cup and light one up while you take in some truly heady tunes.

ZEN
AND THE
ART OF
MAGENITE
SUSPENSION

BY
MIGHTY RAHIEM

Mighty Rahiem

Zen and the Art of Magenite Suspension

Nobody knows why Walt stopped coming back. Sasha says he got sick of dying and decided to stay that way. Sad, really. Towards the end, he seemed like he was starting to enjoy it. Some people say that's the whole point… to get used to it. But they didn't know Walt. He wasn't exactly the type to get used to anything. He seemed dead-set on complaining about pretty much everything, regardless of how minor the inconvenience. It was like his battery. He needed to recharge with negativity just to be himself. Maybe that's what did him in; he had nothing left to complain about. Anyway, he's on Earth now and nothing is bringing him back. When you stop showing up, yer gone for good.

For a little while, the idea was floating around that there is a fixed number of deaths a person has on Zerth. Walt offed himself well over a hundred times before he vanished, so the number must be pretty high. Then there's this guy, Larry Beagle, who says he's done it over a thousand. He's got the bank account to prove it too. The difference between Walt and Larry is that Walt was not a happy person, and Larry is. That's my theory. Walt fixed whatever was broken so he didn't need Zerth anymore. As for Larry, it's a mystery. For me? I don't know. Maybe I just like it here too much. Maybe that's my malfunction.

I'm walking through town on my way to the local Fisher's office with a contract for a few dozen men. With the ocean breeze, the smell of boiled cadkraut carries across the dirt road and mixes with the bounce of **Mountain, by Colour Haze**. The DJ's really got an ear for the mood of the place – and when I say place, I mean everything – the whole planet. I think it's just one guy. He's the one who rigged up all these speakers so he's got a monopoly on everyone's eardrums. Dude must have a lot of money.

Aside from the warbling stereo, the street is pretty quiet. A scowling bugman is sweeping his front porch again. He was sweeping an hour ago when I first came though. The occasional hover-bus, half-loaded with new-spawns are the only traffic. You can always tell the new ones around here. Heads hung low with that look of dread across their face; like they killed someone. They'll figure it out soon enough. Up in Tarqus, the new-spawns are different. They're really violent up there so it's tough for a guy like me to find reliable labor. That's why I like Ghong. The workers don't push back at all. They act like they're obligated to do the work. In fact, I've even found myself talking people down from some of the tougher jobs. We've got tractors for that kind of thing, I say. Still, it's like they want to punish themselves.

Concerning Ghong and the Fishers

Ghong straddles the Paregi river as it empties into the Esconder Sea at Zerth's south-central coast. The name comes from the sound of an upended trash can which was upgraded over time to become the town hall. The town itself is situated at the corners of three regions: to the west is Anu Bardus; to the north and west is Agnay; and to the south, Mike's Hard Peninsula. It's a gathering point for Humans to rally and disperse; voluntarily and involuntarily. It's known for its thriving fishing industry (fishing of Humans as well as fishing of fish) and both industries attract all kinds. In fact, that's why I'm here. Not for the fish, but for the Humans; though I actually did plan on grabbing some lunch before we head out.

Anyway, following the Paregi river about 320 miles north is the Azura spawn point, where humans fall from the sky and splat across the brickwork. It's where Larry Beagle does all his business. It's also where I came from. About 50 miles south of Ghong is Bonzo Beach; another spawn point, where Humans are introduced to Zerth with lungs full of water. It's there that Rubin Walter, the famous daredevil, first spawned in. The ease of travel between both spawn points is what makes Ghong so popular with the Fisher-kings. Even the spawns from Tarqus are sometimes flown in from the north.

Fishers are the work-horses of the labor trade. They set up lawn chairs and linger under bright red parasols, waiting for the terrified newcomers to arrive. They do their best to calm the panicked Humans and offer them jobs, working for meager pay to help with all the new construction. Fishers are paid, on average, about three bucks for each Human they wrangle, and then the Fisher-kings rent them out. The entire industry is built to take advantage of Human labor, and it makes the Fishers rich. Admittedly, I am part of that process. I hire Humans.

Off the street and into the shade, where the townsfolk are more active. Just off Plasmaslave Boulevard, the folks have a nice little outdoor market beneath a big red tarp that covers the whole alley. These things always feel like I'm walking into a circus. Right in front, a lazy broccoli-looking fellow is trying to sell me his used tobacco ashes as fish bait. At least that's what he told me that the first time I came through, but now he's saying it's a remedy for the sniffles. He doesn't remember me. There's a group of sprouts hustling an elderly woman who looks like she could use a drink, and a bugman is arguing with a Morouni girl over the price of copper contacts. I don't think she realizes they can read minds.

The broccoli guy is munching on a twig of celery and I make a dumb remark alluding to cannibalism. He shoots back with another dumb remark about Humans eating monkeys. I tell him that Humans don't eat monkeys and fish don't eat ashes, but I catch myself. This is stupid. I'm arguing with broccoli over the appeal of monkey meat. The absurdity of the situation allows me to push through the market at a speedy pace.

Around the corner, Sasha is waiting for me outside the office of Mr. Grandy Boyle. Boyle is a Fisher-king and he runs the largest operation in Ghong. He's got some competition but nothing serious. He keeps a firm grasp on his monopoly through the use of superior firepower and abundant advertising. He's got bruisers and billboards all over town. As for Sasha, he says he's been feeling under the weather and Boyle told him to wait outside so he wouldn't contaminate the place with all his sneezing. He's got a bit of smudged ash under his nose. He's a communist, so he trusts the hustlers in the market – even the broccoli people.

I say he's a communist, but really, there aren't any of those here. Not in practice, anyway. You can call yourself whatever you want but without the compulsion to live for the state, communists tend to wither into opportunistic ancaps. Just like Sasha. He's dead-set on finding something to worship, something bigger than himself to call leader. All the while, living his life wheeling and dealing in the throes of free market utopia, unaware that his preferred ideology has been dragged to death behind his heels. He's working for me, for God's sake. I suppose it could be worse. He could be an Aerie Loyalist. They all talk like the Empire will someday make a triumphant return to put its boot down on all this mixed-race degeneracy, all the while on the lookout for the next big step forward in Morouni anti-gravity.

Speaking of Morouni anti-gravity, that's why I'm here. Kind of. Eventually we will be needing a ride out of town and there's nothing more fashionable than a flying chariot. Even if it's rusted out and pieced together with stripped bolts. I'm not kidding. Iron, duct tape and hope – that's what makes a Morouni ship work. At least that's the meme. As for the cargo – Humans. Mr. Boyle messaged me with a new batch of workers he pulled off the beach and he wants the standard compensation for the labor. Ten-hundred percent, he says. He's a Morouni and doesn't understand concrete numbers, rather he spits out large demands and is generally happy when I go along with it, regardless of what he is actually getting. He never complains when I swipe my card for 10 bucks a head, so I'm here with the money.

It's not slavery – God no. More like a temp-agency that preys on the unaware. The help comes to their senses sooner or later to realize that they don't actually need to work to survive. For that reason, small towns tend to emerge around mining operations when the workers discover they can just walk off the job and build a house for themselves. Sometimes, they even come back to work under private contracts. That's the best, when they come to work because they *want* to work. At that point they usually aren't working for money; they want raw ore for themselves so they can build things. It works. They get to keep half their haul at the end of the shift, and a few days later they have a new barbecue grill or sculpture or something.

I push through the curtain with Sasha ducking in behind me and we enter Mr. Boyle's office. If you didn't know any better, you might think Boyle was running the world's smallest restaurant, but that's just how the Morouni operate. There's always a grill or steaming wok within arm's reach. Even in the office. Looks like a cadkraut stir-fry. Very tasty. The Morouni are big on Human cuisine since their own is pretty much inedible. At least, that's what I hear. Sasha's head is obscured in the cloud of steam hanging around the ceiling. "Squirrel is good cook. Is like kitchen in old country." Sasha can't help but call Boyle a squirrel. If I were more candid, I would probably do the same. The resemblance is striking.

Concerning Morouni

They're fuzzy little bastards. Well, sometimes they are fuzzy *big* bastards. The big ones are pretty rare, though. They're usually about 3 to 4 feet tall but they can shoot up to 6 feet plus. They've got a strange way about them that reminds me of eastern European gypsies. They have a way of pulling you into their world and subjecting you to their way of living. They are excellent at that; and so casual about it, too. Like they don't even realize you are an alien to their ways. Maybe they just don't care. Anyway, it's difficult to pin down their appearance. While all Morouni are easily recognized as such, their diversity within that category is pretty wild. It's almost easier to classify them as a genus rather than a species. Like, I could say the word "dog" and everyone would have their own idea of what that is – but is it a St. Bernard, or is it a chihuahua? The Morouni are that varied.

Culturally, they are warm and welcoming, but also very strict. Not so much with other races, but they have extremely high standards within their own circles. Fuzzy, alien conservatives. That's what they remind me of. They are diligent workers and quite strong for their size. Very strong, in fact.

Probably just as strong as a Human – though only half the size. The bigger ones are pretty much gorillas. You've got to stay out of their way when they get angry lest you find yourself back on Earth with a bad memory of being ripped in half.

Boyle ashes his cigar in the grill and leans across the desk. He's growling. I think he's trying to intimidate us. "Your men are waiting, Mr. Murphy. Can you pay? I didn't fish Humans from the beach to stand around and gather dust."

"Ten-hundred percent," I reply.

Sasha leans out of the cloud and whispers in my ear, "He asks too much for these men. They are not worth that." I told you he was a capitalist.

Boyle vanishes behind his man-sized desk and emerges around the side. His desk is taller than he is. He leads us through a tight hallway that opens into a fenced-off yard where thirty or so Humans are mulling around. **Afroman – Plastilina Mosh** is pounding on the stereo and I've got my groove on. I miss my afro. I've got this crew-cut-thing now. Maybe I'm due for a haircut. Anyway, Boyle instructs the crew to line up and sound off, and we are introduced to each new member of the team as they shout their first names in order. 22 men and 6 women. They are all terrified. This is normal. They still think they are in hell, so they act as such, giving any semblance of authority the utmost respect. Boyle walks down the line with a switch in his hand, tapping kneecaps as if he's testing their reflexes. "These are good Humans. You pay me top dollar and you get the best!" He says, as if he had any choice in the quality. "The women will breed for you," he says, as he swats the belly of a large woman who breaks into tears.

At this point I have to step in. I pull Boyle aside and close the deal by whipping out my credcard and waving it in his face. His eyes grow wide. Dealing with the Morouni is a chore. You have to put up a front of getting the short end of the stick. They want the feeling of control over you, so you play along and act as if you've just been knocked down a peg. They've all got short-man syndrome. Whatever they are selling, just act as if they've done you a humongous favor. You keep it up and you can get whatever you want. "The price is steep, but fair," I say, feigning hard.

"If it's too steep for you, you can go somewhere else for Humans," Boyle says.

"It's very fair," I say. "And you have my gratitude. Ten-hundred percent, you say?"

"Ten-hundred percent." Boyle whistles.

We finalize the deal with a nod and I swipe my card, transferring 280 bucks to his account. His talkman chirps and he dashes inside without saying a word. Morouni aren't big on casual goodbyes.

I approach the large woman and introduce myself, leading her away to the shade. She's hysterical. I assure her that she is nobody's slave and that she is free to go. I show her how her talkman works and transfer 100 bucks to her account so she has a decent cushion, and I point her in the direction of the nearest tavern. I find that's the best way to acclimate new-spawns who are having a rough time. Booze always does it. She shambles off in a daze but I'm not entirely convinced she's going to be okay.

With the crew assembled and all debts paid, I shoot a message to our ride out of town. His name is Carton and he's our pilot. Another Morouni. I've worked with him several times in the past so we've built a decent working relationship. He's not the most punctual, but let's say he's reliably consistent. That's the best way to put it. He tells me a steamer is en-route to Calibur from Ortega, and we can link up with it to save on fuel. Sounds like a plan. It will add some time to the trip but we're in no hurry. While we wait for our ride, I take the opportunity to introduce myself to the crew. I assure them that they aren't slaves (as I'm morally obligated to do) and that they are free to leave at any time, though if they stay, they will be paid. No one leaves so I continue my spiel. I give them the quick rundown and tell them about the job. It's a construction gig on the east coast, south of Calibur, where some Sluggs have recently begun their own construction of a pumpstation. Sasha interjects with an unsolicited anecdote about working with Sluggs. He's a big fan. I try not to confuse the new-spawns with all the complicated business involving Sluggs vs. Sectoids vs. Morouni vs. Legomi; and where Humans fit into the mix. It's just too much of a hassle. They'll figure it out on their own. What *is* important are the standard units of measurement we all adhere to on Zerth. I do my best to explain.

Concerning Time

The town of Ghong was established in Jubai of the year 121, which threw everyone off. In the early days, there was little consensus concerning the passage of time, seeing as how there are no nights or seasons. After much debate, most were content to fall under the Aerian/Sectoid calculation as it was the only system that held firm to itself.

Each day consists of forty hours, roughly the amount of time it takes for the eleven suns to complete a full cycle. There are a few extra minutes in there but we just ignore them. Days are nested in weeks, much like Earth, though a bit skewed. It seems the Sectoid's efforts to understand Human systems brought about some strange consequences. Monday is Onesday, Tuesday is Twosday, Wednesday was begrudgingly jammed into Threesday, much to the shattered sensibilities of the Sectoids. Thursday is Foursday, even though it sounded better as Threesday, and Friday is Fivesday. Saturday and Sunday were abandoned because they didn't sound like numbers at all and they had already made an exception with Threesday. Five days in a week.

Years were much more difficult to calculate. Aelvus, the Sectoid home planet, is a Dyson Sphere, and therefore has no solar rotation or seasons. Neither does Zerth. Their limited exposure to Earthly passage of time caused all the confusion. Since the Sectoids had nothing to offer in terms of yearly distinction, the Humans stuck to their own understanding. Roughly 8,766 hours per year on Earth, totaling 219 days per year on Zerth.

The concept of months was also borrowed from Humans, though to a lesser degree. The Morouni couldn't handle yet another arbitrary system of measurement, so only six months were adopted, each spanning 36.5 days. Jarruwary, named after some kind of Sectoid god. Febnimary, for the famous brewer of beer, as well as its similarity to February. Mich, named after another Sectoid deity. Jubai, because it sounds like July. Septo, September, and the Septet of Sectoid gods; and Garry, for Garry, the guy that drives the tractor. Yeah, I know, it's ridiculous. He hasn't driven a tractor in years. Last I heard, he was flying deliveries in a pubber.

In short time, Carton arrives in dramatic fashion. The crew ducks for cover as the screams of the engines are heard from a distance, skimming rooftops and sweeping around to give us all a good look at the paint job on the underbelly of his ship. It's a cartoon image of himself with a word-bubble shouting, "Off and Away!" while giving a thumbs up. Years ago, the image led to the nickname "Often Away," as he's a notorious drunk. The name stuck.

"Squirrel is good pilot," Sasha says, wiping his nose and nudging a worker with his elbow. All the Morouni look like squirrels to him, I guess. The machine lands with a bump in the yard and Carton cuts the engines, allowing the dust to settle before making a dramatic departure from the ship's cargo bay.

The Often Away is a modified carrier from the bowels of the world-famous Kaggworks, retrofit with Aerian head-fans for swift travel. Carton designed it himself. He's ahead of the curve when it comes to adapting new technology, which is why I prefer working with him. Given the duality of the design, he essentially pilots the thing like two ships in one. He's got the standard Morouni steamer controls to regulate the temperature of the Polerite cores (think levers and valves) mixed with the high-tech Sectonian thrusters, which rely on an on-board computer for balance. So he plugs away in the cockpit, kicking levers and yanking strings attached to valve-release dials and slapping buttons on a display screen. It's like watching a puppeteer. Lots of fun.

His kids are on board as well. He brings them along on every flight. All 12 of them. Children of the sky. They are sweet little scamps and generally not too much of a hassle. One in particular is great fun. His name is Little Dave and I've never seen his face as he keeps it hidden beneath an adult-sized blast helmet. At first, I thought he was just messing around, but Carton tells me that it's there to protect his brain from the elements. Little Dave was born with a bizarre birth defect called Inverse Cranium, and the helmet is there to keep his exposed brain away from all the dirt in the air. He says it will eventually scab over, but he will always have to wear the helmet. The kid doesn't seem to mind.

We're a pretty bare-bones operation at the moment so we will need to gear up in Calibur before we break ground. The east coast is a notorious hunting ground for

Mercs and it's likely that we'll be raided. That kind of danger is common here, though the word "danger" has taken on a different meaning as I've grown more accustom to life on Zerth. Back home, getting run off the road by a gang of 40 armed bandits and living to tell the tale would probably get you a book deal. It would make the news. Here, it's a minor inconvenience, like forgetting to bring your umbrella in a thunderstorm. It sucks, but it's hardly worth mentioning, unless yer a drama queen… or have nothing else to talk about. But that's the wilderness. Everyone's out to take advantage of you. You get by, simply, by not letting them.

Concerning Self Defense

So, we defend ourselves in any way we feel necessary. Sticks, rocks, swords and particle-beam-cannons. You'd think the rock-chuckers were at a disadvantage, and to some degree they are, but it doesn't take much to knock someone unconscious. Hell, the big seller last year was something called a "leadie." Literally, a lead ball the size of your fist that you heave at your enemy. You'd be surprised at how quickly someone will drop their rifle to get out of the way of one of those things. It could break your knee! Then some other jerk decided to invent the "leadie-launcher". It's a cannon... like an 18th century cast-iron cannon. Nobody could take the backwards irony so it was abandoned to the scrap-heap of history. Somehow, the leadie was not. Anyway, that was last year's big seller. The meme weapon of the season. The pet rock of self-defense. Price tag: a buck.

These things go in cycles. It's really less about the effectiveness of the weapon and more about the surprise factor. As the general sense of self-preservation declines, the focus shifts to theatrics. A while back, the Face-fucker-5000 was really big news. A modified grenade launcher designed to detonate the payload the instant it leaves the barrel, and it requires a combustion engine to function. There's a bit more to it, but the idea is to chase your target around with a rapid burst of controlled explosions. It's got an effective range of about 10 feet and you really should wear gloves while using it. Either way, it sold like hotcakes. Everybody wanted one. Price Tag: 70 bucks.

The Nale series of firearms were developed by the Sluggs and are wholly terrifying. A simple pistol casing equipped with a battery is all they are. The part that makes them so horrifying is the ammunition. Simple shaved bricks of polerite can be locked into the handle and secured. When the trigger is pulled, the battery makes contact with the polerite, liquefying and propelling through the barrel at gut-wrenching speeds. The result is a barrage of super-heated polerite barbs moving at stupid speed. The trigger can even be held down to fire a constant stream, like a water-gun, only much more deadly. Price tag: 3 bucks (though the ammo is considerably more expensive).

So, we've got a casualty. As we were boarding the ship, Charles knocked his head on the overhang in just the right way that he ruptured a vessel in his forehead, shooting blood into the eye of Samantha, who fell backwards into the heat-intake of the craft. It was all so quick that nearly everyone missed it. The only evidence was a pink mist of unknown origin that joined with the dust around the yard. I'm not saying anything. Don't want to freak anyone out.

Yes, there is a lot of death here, but it doesn't hold the same weight. Violence only excites the attention because of its lasting implications. Without those implications, it becomes less of an issue. What's more impacted is my wallet. Not that it's a huge problem; it's easy enough to make back and it's all going to a noble cause. At least, that's how I think about it. I like to think I'm paying for people's freedom. They are scooped up by the Fishers and hassled into servitude, then I show up and offer them a way out. I mean, I'm still putting them to work, but I make sure they know their options. That's not a luxury the Fishers provide.

The cabin of the Often Away is comfortably occupied. We're all moshed together in the leather-fab seats, prepared for takeoff. Sasha has carved out a nice chunk of personal space with his constant sniffling, so his row is particularly squished. There would be more room if it weren't for the pallet of electronics in the front of the cabin. Carton says it's for an important client, but I'm pretty sure I remember it being there the last time I flew with him. That was about a month ago. I think he's just a pack rat.

The radio flicks on to the tune of **Joy Division's Transmission** and everyone's head is bobbing. The cabin dims and the caution lights fill the room with a red glow. The head-fans whir to a steady hum and the natural light of day is obscured by a cloud of dust across the windows. The gurgling of boiled water passes under our feet and up the walls, filling the heat-exchange manifold with steam. The regulators kick in and everything settles to a neutral hum, then a hard hiss and the crew is pushed into their seats as we lift off. The dust is replaced by a swiftly sinking horizon, then blue sky. The cabin is flooded with sunlight as the craft turns eastward and we ease into our ascent. It's like water. I cannot fathom a sweeter ride.

The caution lights kick out, allowing for the natural sun to fill the cabin. Rays of dust crisscross the aisle through the porthole windows, gliding freely through the air, occasionally excited by Sasha's sneezing. The door to the cockpit slides open and in come the children, followed by a well-lit Carton. He's got a flask of the good stuff, which he offers to members of the crew. I take him up on it and down a swig. Rootcasket. Good stuff indeed. A little too good. I hope our pilot doesn't kill us all.

Concerning Cuisine

What do Friday nights look like on Zerth? Aside from being extremely bright, copious amounts of beer. Though "invented" by the Sectoids (aka Human knockoff) It's the Legomi who are the true masters of the brew. The few crops grown outdoors are hops, barley and wheat. Keeping everyone adequately sauced requires more room than private gardens can provide, so great tarps are draped over the crops to keep them from burning. It's everyone's happy responsibility to check on them. After all, without beer, how could they possibly go on? Drinking is so ingrained into Zerth's culture that it's considered unusual to not have at least one or two a day. The concept of drunkenness is akin to sleeping. You are either "on the narrow" (mostly sober) or "on the wobble" (mostly not sober). And if you are on the wobble, you probably shouldn't be doing anything that requires a lot of manual dexterity. It's understood.

Though everyone is always drunk, very few have problems controlling themselves (with the exception of walking straight). No one drinks to escape or to feel sorry for themselves; they drink because it tastes so damned good. The Legomi are to be thanked for that, as the standard plant-man can put down four or five gallons before passing out. If they are to be imbibing that much joy juice, it better taste amazing. That's their thinking. Those that refuse to control themselves are often booted out of town. It's seen as a symptom of a larger problem that no one wants to deal with. Any refusal to leave is answered with bullets. For this reason, bullets are also in high demand.

Aside from booze, the food is always rich. Barbecue is most common – preparing food indoors and cooking out. A single elephant vulture can feed a town of 300 for a week, and if you ever managed to kill one, a macromite can make enough bacon to fill a bus. I say macromite, but in truth they're just tardigrades. Really, really big tardigrades. I have no idea how they got here. Vegetables are much more common than meat, as there is no livestock or anything of the like, though fishing is a big industry as well. Fish and eggs are the most common source of protein and are quite easily gathered by ones self.

Human cuisine is the norm on Zerth. The style, that is. Before we showed up, flavor wasn't even a thing. Traditional Sectoid nutrition is delivered in the form of a spongy paste sans enjoyment, and the Morouni were accustomed to pressed sheets of dried and processed fiber. Think cardboard, but more cardboardy. The Legomi eat anything. Rocks, even. But they were bowled over when they realized they could flavor their rocks. Thankfully, Humans showed up and schooled the planet with our mastery of the culinary arts. I argue that we earthlings take our love of food for granted. We don't realize how amazing we are at eating. Most beings of Zerth don't have a history of enjoying their nutrition, so it's then that you come to terms with how revolutionary it is to enjoy it.

Much to the dismay of every Human, there is no such thing as salt on Zerth. At least it's not naturally occurring. There's Ketchup, but no salt. Pepper, but no salt. Salt is akin to gold. It's one of the main things Humans import regularly, so if you've ever noticed a coworker or family member carrying a salt shaker around in their pocket, there's a good chance that they are a traveler to Zerth. Though it's a staple of Human cuisine, no one else cares much for it – especially not the Sluggs.

About a half-hour into the flight, our steamer comes into view, port-side. A whale of a ship. I have to admit, I have a fascination with these things and it brings me back to my childhood whenever I see one. There's nothing aerodynamic about them at all. Enormous contraptions floating on clouds of steam – like a structural welder's vision of heaven. Instead of the pearly gates, you get raw beams of iron and rebar joining staggered mezzanines, stacked atop each other and forming the rough shape of a warehouse without walls. All of it sitting comfortably on a puff of white smoke. The radio spazzes out and we're treated to **Freedom Run, by Kyuss**. I remember seeing them open for Faith No More back in the day and I've been hooked ever since.

A deep horn blasts, shaking through the cabin and our request to dock is accepted. We pull alongside the iron beast; and, for a moment, the windows go white as we pass through the steam. Through breaks in the cloud, I can see the crew of the giant scurrying across the catwalks the with wheelbarrows of raw ore. Food for the furnace. We pass into shadow and there's an awkward jerk and bump. The crew shifts nervously with the sound of shearing metal to the rear of the ship and the caution light comes back on. Less of a warning and more of a confirmation that things have indeed become bumpy. The shearing crescendos with a thud and the engines cut out. Docking successful. From here to Calibur is 688 miles so we've got about five and a half hours to kill. Steamers aren't exactly speedy travel, but it's a free ride so I can't complain. Sasha expresses his interest in getting some fresh air and I can't blame him. He squeezes through the aisle and we head to the loading ramp at the back of the cabin.

Another casualty. I'm not sure if I can explain it, but I'll try my best. Charles tried to push through the door at the same time as Timothy, who shoved him aside and kicked him in the groin. Charles retaliated, going airborne in Timothy's direction. I guess Greg was caught up in the whole thing and walked right into a post. At first I thought he had just bruised his nose, but no, the fucker is dead. He didn't even fall over. In fact, he's still standing even after we looted his corpse. Never seen anything like it. Either way, he had some really sweet knuckle dusters and an old telescope.

The crew unloads into the mist and we take in the moisture and coolness of the altitude. There's no one here to welcome us so we are free to wander the rear of the steamer unhindered. If you didn't know any better, you'd think you were standing in the skeleton of a rusted-out factory. Like they got half way through building the thing and decided to say screw it, let's make it fly right now. But that's just how Morouni ships work. Fully exposed to the elements. Not that I mind. It's a cool 72° and the damp air is a welcome retreat from the norm. Sasha and I make our way to the port-side railing to take in the view. Through the pockets of steam, an ocean of sand drifts below as the beast lumbers across the northern reaches of Agnay. The ship's captain appears and introduces himself. Yuma Shuma is his name. He welcomes us aboard with that Morouni smile and tells us we are joining the ship on its maiden voyage; a world tour to test the beast's integrity. He says the name of the ship is The Baconator. That's a whole other story, but I'll keep it short and say that the Morouni like to name their ships after the women in their family. For example: The Often Away was originally named Turducken. Anyway, The Baconator disembarked from the Kaggworks in Southtown, traveled up the Meapos Peninsula, and took on some passengers in Ortega. From there, they passed through the northern edge of Anu Bardus and into Agnay, where we linked up.

Concerning Geography

Anu Bardus, the home of the great burning basin, is where the Sectoids first landed their tower. It's the largest region of Zerth, and not home to much of anything besides Aerie Tower and a scant few mining operations.

Despite its relative lifelessness, the southern extremities of Anu Bardus are rich with green fields and farmlands. A good amount of Zerth's agriculture is found in this area. The name Anu Bardus means First Power in Aleven, the Sectoid native tongue.

Agnay, the heart of Zerth, is even more desolate. For most of its area, nothing lives except the occasional roaming flocks of sand-squid, who by all recollection, are really just doing their best to pass through. The northern quarter of the region bumps up against the Paregi river, which gives way to the fertile Erebo highland shelf, before dropping in altitude and becoming the northern pool of the burning basin. As for the heart, the heat is too much to handle for all but the sturdiest of travelers, as it's the only region where the influence of the eleven suns are felt at all times.

Mike's Hard Peninsula is named after the same alcoholic beverage created by Anthony, the engineer who helped found Ghong. No one argued with him over the name as it seemed strangely appropriate. The majority of the peninsula is made up of the foothills and peaks of the Mike's Hard Mountain Range, which rises up along the eastern coast. The west coast of the peninsula gives way to Esconder

Sea, and the east coast opens up to the great ocean. The Peninsula is home to the famous Mike's Hard Port Town, whose main export is the processed sugar extracted from the pools along the coast.

The Meapos Peninsula makes up a significant chunk of the western coast of Zerth, jutting out of the northern portion of Red Rock. While its western coast boasts some of the most unforgiving terrain, the remainder offers a pleasantly hospitable environment. Being quite distant from the heart of Zerth, the climate of Meapos maintains a sunny, but cool, 82° year round; and the relatively high amount moisture allows Meapos to thrive as Zerth's king of agriculture. At the southern tip of the peninsula is the bustling and diverse Rabbit City; one of Zerth's most populace centers, specializing in sea trade and technology, as well as being home to historic Southtown. The Kaggworks are here as well.

Red Rock shares the western coast with Meapos. It's named for the dense redrock stone that is abundant in the area, which is prized for its durability and crafting applications. It's like to marble in composition. The region is host to thousands of bluffs, cliffs and canyons overseeing the western portion of the burning basin. The town of Ender, nestled within the Georgio Gorge, is the oldest settlement of Zerth, which now enjoys year-round tourism, thanks to its marvelous architecture and enduring charm. Red Rock is rich with minerals, from Polerite to coal to gold and silver, though its most lucrative export is Magenite. At the base of the Amber Cliffs is the Magfarm – the largest source of refined Magenite. Due to the volatility of the ore, they had to build the whole thing in a faraday cage and extract it by hand. No electricity allowed, as the properties of the mineral would cause the entire place to implode with a strong enough current. There's plenty more to talk about, but the fact is, there's quite a bit that hasn't been explored yet.

The Baconator lets out a blast of steam and the lower deck is engulfed in a hot, wet cloud as the ship gains altitude. The fog clears and we're all soaked. It's a necessary maneuver as we are passing over the Katarri mountain range. Passing over isn't really the right way to put it. Passing through is more accurate. Some of the peaks are higher than we are. The captain treats us to a view of the forested crags as we lumber dangerously close to the cliff-sides. "Squirrel is good captain," Sasha says. I don't know, the guy looks more like a rabbit to me, but whatever. Yuma skillfully disregards the remark and goes on telling us about his family. He's got 30 kids on the way. Jesus Christ. He says the ship was his wedding dowry from his sister. I make an off remark about how her family must be pretty loaded and he tells me that it's tradition for the bride to offer the dowry. I find a way to keep my mouth shut.

The radio kicks into **Godless by The Dandy Warhols** and the mood shifts so goddamned abruptly that I have to walk away. This is music for the individual. Cannot be heard in groups. Not properly anyway. I find a spot beneath the hull on a hanging mezzanine and take in the view. The casual wail of the trumpet echoes off the stone and the leaves brush across the bottom of the walkway. The trees are so close I can touch them. It's times like this that I can truly take advantage of my loss of self-preservation and just enjoy the ride. We might crash. Who cares. The experience is stronger than a thousand deaths and I gladly put myself in hazard's way to be a part of it. Just pull it all in. Inhale it.

The Katarri mountains are the adopted home of the Sluggs. They've got good taste. Probably the only area of Zerth with an actual forest; though I'm told it wasn't always this lively. The Sluggs plopped a pumpstation atop Mt. Katarri and let the thing drain into the basin, flooding the whole place. It's an area roughly the size of Delaware. The result is an oasis of dense forest and rushing water – like veins down the mountainside. It reminds me of the trip to Cancun that I never took. The wife wanted it, but the wallet said no.

I do have a family – and yet I don't. On Earth, my wife and two kids have no idea where I am. I don't see them until some catastrophic event tears my body apart and I'm whisked away to that place again as if no time has passed at all. Years fly by and yet they don't. The first time I went back I was convinced it was all a dream. I told everyone about it and they thought it was great fun... until I ran into someone who had the same dream. Not exactly the same, but close enough. He was here. He is here. Somewhere. His name is Dean and he dreams about drowning. I dream about falling. We both belong here. My family doesn't and they have no clue what I'm talking about. I'm not sure I want them to. It's a terrible thing to face.

It's not some kind of schizophrenic fantasy – living two lives at once – my mind doesn't work that way. You only have one home and Earth now feels like a hospital. It's the place you end up when something has gone seriously wrong. I know how backwards that sounds, but here, I am who I am. There, I'm just Murphy.

I'm an engineer by trade, which means something. I mean, it means more than it does on Earth. Back home, my degree afforded me a cubicle and the responsibilities of approving customer blueprints. Sometimes I would write a program for the waterjet, but that was only if the senior engineers weren't around to do it. Here, I can do what I always dreamed of doing. I didn't get a degree in engineering to be locked away and hounded by a boss. Nobody does that. I mean, primarily, I got it to make money doing something I enjoy. It's how you live, right? Well, here things are different. Money flows and no one is worried about making rent or putting food on the table. That much is a given.

On Zerth, I'm able to use my talents to effect change in the way I always dreamed. Here, I feel like a kid again. I can build things that matter. I can build things that people use. The thought of returning to Earth to have all that energy squandered is just crippling. It's like I tell all the guys; on Earth, I make eleven bucks an hour – on Zerth, I make magic. **Planet Z – Buzzhead Republic**. It's confirmed. I'm where I belong. The DJ is awake and staring.

The thing about Zerth is that it's brutal to inventors, but also a million times more rewarding... if you have the right frame of mind. On Earth, it can take decades of your life and thousands, if not tens of thousands of dollars to bring your idea to fruition, just to have a shot at convincing someone else that it's worth everyone's time. If it's worthwhile, you are allowed to enter the lottery of good ideas. If you are lucky, and I mean really lucky, you might be the one in a million that actually makes enough money from your idea that you become rich and famous. It's a crap-shoot. On Zerth, you can do the exact same thing in a fraction of the time and you can do it for free. And there's no lottery. There's also no money or fame. How could there be? Unless it's something I can physically hold in my back pocket, how could I possibly protect it from being stolen? Here, ideas belong to the world. Yeah, I know how that sounds, but it's not because someone made it that way – it's the product of anarchy. There's no one around to tell people *not* to steal it. What am I gonna do? Tell everyone *not* to use my idea? They'd shoot me.

Concerning Technology and Trade

With the great melting pot coming together, standards in technology were proposed. Though everyone had their own idea of what worked best for them, it was a much more difficult question to answer what worked best for everyone. Talkmans are universally accepted as are hyperbikes, hover-buses and the like. But for everything else, there is the UP-port. I designed the UP-port for all things extra. The Universal Peripheral Port (or UPP) allows all technology a common theme. While Morouni steamers lurch through the sky and Sectonian hyperbikes dart about, all are outfitted with Up-ports.

They share a basic design and aspect ratio. Trapezoidal rings with one or two connections for power and information to be relayed. The structure is molded plasteel with Magenite clamps. The UPP-1 is the standard port – exactly 10 inches long at the base and 6 inches long at the top, as well as the height. 10"x6"x6". The UPP-2 is a bit larger, at 15 inches at the base. 15"x9"x9". Not all UP-ports are so small. The largest UPP port is the UPP-20, which is roughly the size of a bus. They're used for everything. Houses, doors, trash-cans, weapon-pods, spare thrusters. All of it is built with the UPP standard, and they're incredibly easy to manufacture. Not to toot my own horn, but the standard UPP is far too convenient for anyone to deviate and expect to thrive.

While on the subject of technological development, intellectual property rights are not only nonexistent, but the entire notion was spat on at the moment it was brought up, by the Sectoids of all peoples. If Group X designs a better stabilizer, Group Y has full rights to copy and manufacture the item. Says who? Says nobody. Nobody is also the same person who says you own your ideas. Monopoly is impossible, and the whole system truly only leads to further improvements. Morouni and Humans argued hotly over the notion; but, in the end, who exists to regulate? Again, nobody.

The Morouni settled on their own morals and held firm. If a new technology came along, the Morouni refused to have anything to do with it unless developed by another of their own kind. On the other hand, modified Morouni technology is generally scoffed at, being a bastardization of their own perfect creation. For this reason, many Morouni settlements tend to brush closer to poverty. That, and the idea that competition in business is a sin.

Morouni aside, intellectual property went out the window, ushering in a boom in technology, much to the surprise of many Humans who claimed the opposite would happen. Claims that no one would have any reason to produce something new if they weren't guaranteed a profit fell apart all too quickly. No one has a regular job. No one earns a monthly wage. All there is to do is tinker and explore. It's the natural reaction to a world of infinite possibilities and many a staunch conservative Human refuses to accept that fact.

Free trade is just that – free. Arguments to the contrary are dismantled by reality. If one were to claim that one could not survive as a small business in such a diverse market, one would be lying to themselves. The answer to the question lies in the question itself. Diversify. If you can't make money because someone stole your idea and sold it better than you, why not rip off your own idea instead and sell it for less. Better yet, sell a better product. Without lawsuits and regulations clogging up the zeitgeist, ideas and new inventions come along every day. That's how we thrive. Allow me to illustrate.

<u>Example A:</u>

Herbert Blinkbottom built a better head-fan for his hyperbikes. Bigby Shitknuckle spied on him and started selling rip-off fans the day before Herbert's hit the market. Herbert found his design for head-fans being used all over town without him selling a single one. Herbert has several options to deal with the situation.

A: Consider the development a success, as everyone now uses it. Money was not his main objective so he is content either way.

B: Consider the theft a personal attack and a detriment to his well-being. He will nuke Bigby's store and everyone in it.

C: Consider his own stolen property to be inferior to what he can produce next – being more careful to guard his design until he can make some money off it.

D: Develop intentionally faulty equipment knowing

that his next project will be stolen by Bigby, and oust him publicly the next time he does it.

E: Go home defeated, never to produce anything ever again because it will just be stolen by someone else who has better marketing skills.

F: Jab Bigby in the groin for his subterfuge and then offer a partnership. Bigby sells the products that Herbert develops.

Example B:

Jenny Nippletwist started a new band and wants to rake in the cash. Her band, Nippletwister and the Noobs, spend hundreds of bucks to record an album in the studio. The album is recorded and doesn't sell at all. Jenny goes mad wondering why nothing sold, only to bite her lip off to find that everyone and their brother is listening to her songs without paying for them. How can Jenny recoup her costs?

A: Personally threaten each individual freeloading her music, demanding fair pay.

B: Call it a mistake, never making music again.

C: Accept that everyone loves her, though she will never get anything for all her efforts.

D: Perform publicly for a price, making money off of the ticket sales. The album could be considered promotional material.

E: Scream "There oughta' be a law" and attack anyone who doesn't agree.

Example C:

Franz McBean brews the perfect beer. He calls it Bubblin' Brown and it flies off the shelf quicker than he can brew it. Jimmy Thehand wants to butt in on the action and make some profit for himself, branding his own beer with the Bubblin' Brown logo. Franz enters a local bar to discover his brand name plastered across some decidedly shitty beer. Franz wants to protect the validity of his booze and so he has a few options.

A: Track down Jimmy and wring his neck until he dies.

B: Rebrand his beer to include "the original" across the label, thus starting a never-ending battle with the copy-cat.

C: Allow the name to be dragged through the mud and give up.

D: Allow the name to be dragged through the mud and make a newer, better beer.

E: Propose a truce with Jimmy and go into business together.

F: Accept the possibility that a brand name will always be subject to theft and therefore rely on his own personal beer-fame to sell unmarked beer to the people closest to him.

The correct answers may not be entirely clear, but for Zerth, the name of the game is adaptation. The world wasn't built with rules to make things easier, it was built *without* rules to make the most of it all. Only those with the limited vision to consider failure a finality are the ones doomed to allow their mistakes to kill their aspirations. On Zerth, failure isn't really a thing at all – only misguided hopes are a thing. If one truly thought they could make a buck selling something in a world where anything can be so easily duplicated... well, reality strikes. Then, the question becomes, why make anything at all? The answer is clear. They shouldn't, but for some asinine reason, they do anyway. Maybe, in some deep corner of their unconscious thinking, the financial opportunities afforded by creating something never actually occurred to them; and, in reality, they just wanted to create anything... for the hell of it. Then, someone likes what they created and wants to give them money for it. Huzzah!

The issue is the rigorous Earth thinking. Everyone's got bills to pay and mouth's to feed, so we do our best to monetize our hobbies; or, at least monetize the things we can stand doing. For the people of Zerth, building something is rarely a means to an end, only a means to alleviate the gnashing agony of stagnation. The truth of the matter is, no one on Zerth cares if their inventions are stolen. They will never run out of food, water or shelter, and nothing they create is ever relied on for survival. Don't believe me? I invented the UPP port and I've seen *zero* payout for any of it... zero *monetary* payout that is. There's a break in the thinking when you see all the good your ideas have done. There's always that lingering thought of "hey, why didn't I get paid for this?", but that's quickly overruled with the notion that you didn't pay a dime for your home or your food... or anything you need. It's all the little things that cost money, and even those are easily duplicated by hand, if you were so inclined.

I know what you're thinking. Everything is free. No, everything is not free. If I wanted a house, I could build it myself with whatever was laying around or I could take the simple route and buy one. Is food free? If you catch it yourself it is. Otherwise, you can toss a buck to the fish market guy and get lunch. Money is the great equalizer on Zerth. Those who can't or wont do the work will get money and have someone else do it for them. I may sound callous when I say that, but it's the truth here. Say an elderly man can't perform manual labor. He will undoubtedly be collecting donations for spouting wisdom. It's how things work here. Money is akin to smiles and laughter on Earth. If you approve of something, you toss a buck or two.

Is there poverty? Absolutely. Those who are bad with money are those bad with social skills. They either gave too much away or let themselves be conned out of their earnings. What to do when you find yourself at rock bottom? Anything. Go hang out at a flight tower and start moving boxes. No one is there to tell you not to, and with each job you finish, you get to swipe your card.

I don't mean to confuse anyone, so I'll break this down as simply as possible for those who are still in the haze. It's not as obtuse as it may seem. The ability to produce + labor = a product. That product can be sold or rented. Simple as that. Where do the raw materials come from? The ground you stand on. Where does the knowledge come from? Either trial and error or by watching those who already put in the effort. Factories don't mass produce as they do on earth. They build machines and rent them out. What about personal injury as a result of incompetent operation of said machinery? I've died a dozen times and it hasn't stopped me from being an imbecile around a break-press, but I have learned that I shouldn't stand inside the thing as it bends a sheet of steel.

Don't mistake what I am saying. These ideas *cannot* work on Earth. It's a sad reality that we address every morning, as we wake up and shamble into the office in a daze. Our existence relies on our ability to perform out of necessity. Not so on Zerth. The only necessity here is the strength and fortitude to pull yourself back to your feet after you get bowled over. You will be bowled over daily, but none of it is threatening to your livelihood in any way. The only consequence of failure is the necessity of admitting that you fucked up and now you have to start over. That's it. That's all there is to it.

Concerning Wealth

If you're wondering where all this money came from, your guess is as good as mine. There's a theory that some shadowy figure at the top is controlling our wealth, which is probably true – but he has yet to go public about it. The thing is, dropping the practice altogether wouldn't be that big of a hassle. The evil super-villain has no grip… if that is what's actually going on. What I do know is that there is a set amount of money in the world. There's an equal amount that is slowly funneled in to protect against deflation. Who does this? Probably the super-villain. I don't know.

You see, I'm one of the few fortunate enough to have been around since the fall of the Aerie Empire. There was a good decade or so where barter was the only means of trade. Barter still works just fine now, but about ten years after the fall, money showed up. None of it is physical, it's all just numbers in a computer tied to your cred-card. When you pay for something, the seller swipes your card and types in the amount he is charging you. If you're wondering about theft, it does happen; but, then again, so do retaliatory shootings. If some dick charges me 5,000 bucks for some socks, I'm going to shoot him. He doesn't want that to happen so things stay civil.

There is also a form of debt. Credit, I guess. You can make electronic promissory notes which you pay off by feeding your account money. It's a weekly thing. If, after 5 days, your account shows no positive activity, you are dinged and go into the hole a little deeper. Who set this all up? Probably the super-villain. I do my best to stay out of that kind of debt, but many don't. What happens if you don't pay at all? Well, that's a whole other story. A whole other industry, if I'm wanting to be accurate. Slavery exists here, but I'll leave it at that.

The forest is behind us and it's back to an empty brown canvas accompanied by **Electric Sex Circus – Spanner Badge**. Never heard of em, but the DJ says he's a fan. He says there's more to come. As I look over the railing I can see the banks of the Smando river down below – and beyond, the tail end of the Oroouro Ridge. Another half-hour or so and we'll be in Calibur. Airspeed is a steady 120mph in a south-southeastern heading at an altitude of 8,000 ft. I love my talkman. It tells me everything. Carton shows up with a request to return to the Often Away. He says he's called ahead and reserved a parking spot so he doesn't want to waste any time in getting there. We follow him back to the dock where our crew is shuffling up the ramp, and we once again pack ourselves into the sardine can.

A few minutes pass and the caution light blips on, followed by a series of thumps and bumps. All at once, my head hits the wall as our pilot releases the docking clamps before he's even warmed up the engine. The wall is now the floor and we are in free-fall. The head-fans aren't even running. We're all going to die. The workers are freaking out and tumbling over each other in the aisle. It's chaos. Sasha yells at me through the turmoil. He wants to know if he dies, will he still have a cold when he comes back. I tell him I don't know, but I don't think he can hear me. I begin making mental preparations for returning to Earth. This is a real a hassle.

Our third casualty. Charles crawls to the back of the ship and is trying to open the airlock. I have no idea what he's trying to do, but his boot knocks the fire extinguisher off the wall and sends it dancing through the cabin, covering everyone in white foam and bouncing off the head of McGuiness, who soils himself. Not sure what happened to Nancy, but she died. Maybe she's allergic to the foam. I don't know. Lewis must be Catholic because he's made his way over to Nancy's body and is reading her her last rights. I'm not sure how that kind of thing works here. Catholicism, that is.

The engine spits to a start and the head-fans kick on. We all land in a pile at the back of the cabin as our pilot finally decides to *fly his ship*. Everyone's pissy and I've got foam in my mouth. Sasha's pissy because he didn't die. He was really counting on coming back without the sniffles. Too bad for him. He can die on his own time if he wants. Anyway, we all get situated and take a moment to loot Nancy's body. She had some nice sunglasses and a leather fanny pack.

So, the ship rights itself and no one cares to take their seats. We're all pretty shaken up. Through the windows I can see the rooftops of Calibur and the communications kiosk of the flight tower coming up on the starboard side.

I can see why Carton wanted to get here quickly; it's a madhouse. There's a long line of ships waiting to dock and I'm not sure how much Carton paid the flight master to get bumped to the head of the line, but it must have been significant. Maybe he called in a favor.

We pull a strange maneuver and sweep around the north side of town, dropping to an altitude of about 30ft. Looks like Carton is going for another dramatic entrance. The rooftops are mostly above us as we approach the tower, allowing for the voyeur in me to intrude on the daily goings on of the people of Calibur. Zerth has yet to adopt the concept of insurance so when Carton clips the corner of someone's house, nobody pays for it. It's not seen as wise or acceptable to do so, but it happens nonetheless.

A bit of zig-zagging and hull-checking and we're all getting used to the bruises, but we do manage to find a spot in line. Carton says the dock we're waiting for should be available in about 15 minutes. The guy ahead of us (a hot dog vendor) paid for the spot for two hours but Carton's slick dealing overruled. The hot dog guy will let us dock and unload in his spot as long as the Often Away is out of the way within 10 minutes. That's got to be pretty weird for the people waiting to buy a hot dog.

The interior of the flight tower was intended to function as arrival/departure gates, like the airports on Earth. I know this because I designed them (more on that later). What ended up happening was more like the food court in a mall. Imagine trying to board your airplane and you're walking down the jetway, but instead of a plane at the end, it's some jerk with a kebab stand. He tells you that you don't want to fly today and that you want to buy his kebab. You say you have places to be and you don't want any of his damned kebab, but your plane is nowhere to be found because the kebab guy caught wind of the whole thing prior and shot the pilot and stole his plane and turned it into a kebab stand. That's Zerth. You don't get used to it as much as it stops surprising you.

So, it's been 20 minutes and the hot dog guy isn't moving. From the looks of it, Carton has lost his patience and we're now rapidly gaining altitude. I have no idea what he's doing. He sets down on the loading dish of the tower as a gaggle of bugmen come running in our direction, waving their hands and cursing. We aren't supposed to park here. It's meant for pick-up and drop-off of goods, but here we are, stationary in the loading zone. Despite the detriment to our situation, I find myself wondering if anyone's bothered to invent the Zertian equivalent of a tow truck. I guess not. I pop my head into the cockpit for answers and Carton tells me he will meet us outside of town in an hour, and that he isn't supposed to park here. No shit. He says to unload the crew and just act cool.

Departure has us staring down an angry crowd of Sectoids demanding we stay put. The radio is blasting **Butthole Surfers – Who Was In My Room Last Night**, and the atmosphere is equally hostile. I couldn't feel more out of place. We've got guns pointed in our direction and none of us are armed... well, Sasha is armed. I make sure everyone knows Sasha is armed. Sasha is blowing his nose in his sleeve. We need a quick escape. Not much would keep this mob from painting the walls with our faces if things get ugly. The lead bug is probing my brain. Quick – think of something calm and soothing. No use, they're all laughing at me. Goddamn this music. Sasha jumps into action and waves his pistol around and the bugs retaliate. I hit the deck as shots ring out and the whole place lights up with green flickers of plasma. The workers dive for cover as the Often Away abandons us, blasting dust across the ground. The smoke is blinding; I can't see a damned thing. Just bolts of green death flashing around me and Sasha's in the middle of it, popping off shots with his 9mm.

"Wait! I have idea!" Sasha shouts, and the gunfire comes to an abrupt halt. I can barely make out Sasha lumbering through the haze. He's so damned casual. "Murphy is engineer," he says. "He builds tower for you to work. He comes here to inspect tower. He is boss." I see where he is going with all this and play along. Given my role in developing these things, I've got access to parts of the tower that others don't, so I wave my badge to the bugmen and make my intentions known. Sure, they can read your mind, but that doesn't mean you can't lie to them. It's just got to be partially true. The Sectoids invade my brain once again and I put up a front of authority. Thank god it works. The bugs calm down and tell us to sit tight until they can figure something out with their supervisor. I'm willing to wait if it means we all get out of this alive. You get that a lot with Sectoids. They can shift on a dime. One moment, they are shooting at you – the next, they are filling out paperwork. Though you never get an apology.

Concerning Sectoids

The Sectoids – or bugmen, as I affectionately refer to them, aren't the easiest people to get along with. I think it has something to do with their civilization collapsing. Despite that fact, I think it's less about the destruction of order and more about the forced inclusion of everyone else. They would be perfectly happy on their own – but no, we all had to show up. Thankfully, they aren't as hostile towards Humans. In fact, I think they idolize us in a weird kind of way. They go to such great lengths to look and talk just like us that it's kind of endearing when they criticize you. It's like you can tell they are just begging for attention.

The funny thing is, Sectoids don't lie. I don't know if they aren't capable of it or if they just choose not to, but I bet being telepathic has something to do with it. For the same reason, a Sectoid will not hesitate tell the truth, which can get really annoying when they insult you. When a bugman calls you a "Standard, load-bearing imbecile – not worthy of your mother's milk," you know they genuinely don't like you. It's a very candid culture.

Despite the venomous behavior, they can be incredibly handy. They are ridiculously efficient in everything they do. The example here at the flight tower is a good indicator of how they work. It's rare to have a lone Sectoid showing up for a job; rather, you will find 5 or 6 in a tight-knit group – prepared for maximum cohesive productivity. They have high expectations and a rigorous work ethic. It's not at all uncommon for a crew of bugs to take over an employer's business while they are on the job. Not because they intend to, but because it *must be* their way and *only* their way while they work. If you let them do their thing, you won't be disappointed.

Anyway, it's about mid-day now. The loading dish is quiet and the bugs are all away – presumably on lunch. The crew is settled down and taking in the sights. It's a lovely view up here. Tallest building in town. Down below, the city goes about its business with a casual buzz and I find myself feeling grateful for this odd situation that's stuck me above it all. Quite the unique perspective. The homes and businesses with all their bits of personality… it's unfortunate that we only allow ourselves these moments of peace until we don't have a choice otherwise.

Concerning Housing

Most homes are rough, adobe style mud huts, called dobies. (a miscombobulation of adobe) A dobie is a three to four room structure with a bedroom or two, a kitchen, a restroom and a common area. Though some opt for more opulent living, the dobie is the standard. Doors are mostly open walkways, including the front door. This allows for the free air to blow through and keep things cool. For privacy purposes, bright red curtains are hung as covers over entryways and windows. Hobby-dye is plentiful, as the sap of the common hobby tree is boiled down and dried into a fine powder. Add some water and a bit of oil and you have the brightest fire-engine red dye – the ubiquitous color of the doors and windows of Zerth.

The standard dobie construction consists of carbon-fiber mesh nets, much like chicken wire, dipped in pits of tap and allowed to cure. Then, they're propped up as walls and linked together with plasteel rods. Tap is a mix of five parts water, three parts sand and one part plastanite powder. The plastanite allows one gallon of mud to expand to about five gallons, making the already plentiful resources seemingly unlimited. One bag of plastanite provides enough tap for over 70 houses. The tap mixture also keeps the wall-forms extremely light and durable, as well as a perfect insulator from the heat. Floors are fired tap tiles, stained in a variety of browns, golds, or silvers, and set checkered in mud bases. The slick sheen of the tile keeps cool in the shade and allows for a pleasant barefoot experience.

The plumbing is a standard condenser set atop the roof, which drains into a Munda-duct within the upper walls of the exterior, much like a gutter. The Munda-duct flows above all the interior walls in the house and can be tapped and drained anywhere one wishes to have running water. All water runs continuously and is pumped back into the Munda-duct when unused, maintaining a constant cycle. Munda vines are planted within the Munda-duct,(hence the name) which acts as a natural filter for any contaminants picked up during the cycle, as well as granting a faint minty taste to the water.

Restroom facilities are simple steel troughs powered by the main water cycle of the house. Munda vines and winegrass are planted within and allowed to grow out of control, making all "toilets" seem more like giant planters. It keeps the odor to a minimum and allows for contaminants to be purified or destroyed. Any leftover waste is washed into the garden to be used as fertilizer.

Gardens are standard in all homes, big or small. Usually located on the other side of the restroom wall, the garden is the primary source of vegetables for the people of Zerth. Growing vegetables outdoors is an exercise in burnt futility, as the suns never set, so indoor growing is the preferred method. The Munda-duct drains into a latticed irrigation system, feeding between four and ten types of vegetation. The spout is typically decorated with carvings of folded hands, giving forth the bubbling water, though some opt for the vomiting devil face or the flaccid wang design.

Some opt for open plumbing, making all interior walls not quite reach the ceiling. This allows for the exposed Munda-duct to be seen and heard throughout the home. The style is called open-munda, due to the reaching vines allowed to creep across the ceiling and upper walls, giving the interior a nice green canopy. The ducts in the floors are also exposed, allowing for the water to flow across the base of the walls, and even through walkways. Small carbon-fiber bridges are set over the ducts for decoration, featuring floral patterns, faces or hands. Open-munda is available for anyone who wishes for their home to bare a resemblance to an indoor garden.

Furnishing the homes is entirely up to the occupant. Wood is available in small quantities from the stunted hobby tree, but is a rarity as they take so long to regrow. Hobby tree wood is incredibly tough, akin to oak, and is ideal for tables and chairs. Warpood is equally as rare, but is quite brittle and incredibly difficult to shape, as it always wants to warp back to its original form. For that reason, it's used for corks and latices, rather than anything load bearing. Glass is the choice for decoration, stained or otherwise, though glass windows are considered incredibly dangerous. Too many drunks diving out of too many windows keeps glass firmly where it belongs – over the hearth, in shapes of animals and plants.

As we wait, a pubber pulls up and starts unloading. The bugmen jump to attention and get to work, zipping around on their flying forklifts. The properties of magenite are truly astounding. I find myself entertaining the mad scientist in me as I watch the little blips of electricity arc off the magenite blocks at the base of the mast. Oh hell, another casualty. Charles stumbles into the head-fan of the pubber, taking his arm clean off at the elbow and hurling it into the crowd of workers. It hits Stacy in the temple and she's knocked unconscious, tumbling over the side and into traffic where she lands squarely on a pallet of black powder kegs, which detonate, frightening some school children who are passing by. At the same time, some asshole comes up and shoots Lewis in the head. These things happen, I suppose. Luckily, we aren't too bad off as the guy who shot Lewis is also looking for a job. We are putting him in charge of security as he says he's pretty good with a gun. He's a rough looking dude in his mid-thirties with a cleft chin, and something about his eyes tells me he can handle himself. He can be funny at times but he's not as charming as he thinks he is. Sasha doesn't trust him.

The Supervisor finally shows up and leads us to the service elevator. After a bit of haggling he agrees to let us use it. He's a bug with nothing better to do than screw with Humans who need his help. Actually, I think that's a pretty appropriate description of all Sectoids. You just can't argue with them. He makes us address him as "Master". We are all at a disadvantage so I toss the asshole a few bucks per head and load up. The bug slaps the thing into slow-mo and we move at a staggering one-half mile per hour. My talkman says so.

At this pace, we will get to floor level sometime next week. The bug is laughing at us, and he continues laughing for the next 15 minutes. The radio cycles through a handful of songs before we hit the floor, but we finally exit to the tune of **Clinic – Sun And The Moon**. A bittersweet apology for everything we've endured. I swear, this DJ is watching us.

We pile out of the tower and into the light. Central Calibur. It's the closest I've seen to an actual Earthly city. Myopic foot traffic spilling into the road to such a degree that vehicular traffic is useless. Across the street, the Starlight bar and grill is hosting some kind of event involving cosplay. I hope it's cosplay. Either way, I always found the name to be out of place. Most people here have never seen a star, nor would recognize one if they did. Artifacts of Earthly life tend to creep through from time to time and I cant shake the feeling that I'm in a dream. It's almost too natural to be real – if that makes any sense.

I take a headcount of our party before we plunge into the crowd. We're down to 22 workers. I thought we had 26... or 25. I don't know. This is too much for me to deal with, so I hand the reigns over to the guy who shot Lewis. I give him directions out of town where Carton is going to pick us up. It's just outside the city walls, about a 15 minute walk – maybe 20 with all this traffic. He seems eager enough; what could go wrong? The crew shuffles off with the guy who shot Lewis in the lead and Sasha and I head to the market for supplies.

As we walk, Sasha points out a store he wants to check out. Fodroy's Outfitters. He says their prices are always low, as in Always Low Prices. He stresses the syllables as if reciting a poem. I've heard of Fodroy's before but I was under the impression they were based in South Town. A Zertian franchise maybe? Very cool. The storefront is very Earthy as well. It's got real glass windows. That's not normal. And they're plastered with big starburst stickers advertising big deals. Kevlar vests – 20 for 20. Maybe we can make this our one-stop shop.

Heading inside, we're greeted at the door by an elderly man in a lawn chair wearing flight goggles. I expected some kind of verbal greeting, like "Welcome to Fodroy's, can I get you a basket?" but instead he just raises his hand and says "Yo." The dude's a genuine bad ass. I swipe my card and toss the old codger a buck. He deserves it.

The music is different in here. It's not the typical head-rock everyone else is playing, rather a dinky jingle on repeat. Elevator music. Gotta find those Kevlar vests.

Fodroy's is pretty great. It's like a K-Mart. Despite the fact that I vastly prefer Zerth over Earth, it is nice to be reminded of the things I enjoyed in my prior life. Shopping on Zerth tends towards a loose idea of what you need, and an approximate facsimile is sold to you. Sometimes you want boots, and the guy sells you Birkenstocks. Any shopping around will yield similar results as they all get their stock from the same producer and are trying to offload it as quickly as possible. But here, everything I need is right in front of my face. I don't have to ask for anything.

As I browse the aisles, I find myself a nice pair of socks. Argyle even. Score! Sasha comes dashing around the corner with a pair of saw blades. "They will never exbect the blades!" he says, "and brice is so low, is rock bottom!" I ask him what his plans are and he tells me he's going to dual-wield them. Works for me. Maybe he'll start a new fad. I suggest that he get a thick pair of gloves to go with them, but he dismisses me with a scoff. "I will nod be needing widey baby gloves." I think he meant to say whiny baby, but his cold is getting worse.

We continue browsing and I come across a sale on spiked clubs. They're really just baseball bats with nails driven through them, but hey, whats the difference? 20 for 20. That's a hell of a deal. I send Sasha to grab a shopping cart. The next aisle over and there are some helmets. PVC helmets, but who can complain. "One size fits you" is scribbled across each helmet in black sharpie. Another 20 for 20! We snatch up our Kevlar vests and we're good to go.

The cashier is an old blue-haired lady. There's a lot of those on Zerth. You'd be surprised. I flip out my credcard and pay for my supplies. 60.80. Not a bad haul! I wait at the door for Sasha who seems to be trying to make a deal with the old woman. He's got that smile on his face. "I give you 6 bucks for saw blades. Is rock bottom deal. You will take good deal," he says. The lady lights up and he swipes his card. Sasha the haggler. We're good to go.

As we walk outside, I point out the sticker on the window. Sawblades, 20 for 20. They were only a buck a piece. Sasha stares at it for a moment. I tell him better luck next time, but he's not having it. He's gone full-blown berserk. "Capitalist Pigs!" I leave my cart and chase him into Fodroy's where he's making a mess of the place. He dashes down an aisle and shoots left, leaving a trail of destruction in his wake. I do my best to catch up but I'm dodging swords and knives. Two aisles over and I can hear him, sneezing and shouting with the crash of ceramic cookware to the tune of Girl from Ipanema. I round the corner to see him behind the cashier's desk. He's mashing the old woman's face into the register. "Capitalist American Dogs!" There's no way I can stop him.

So, now we're running away now. I'm pushing the cart as fast as I can down High Street as Sasha clears a path ahead of me. I don't dare turn around. I'm sure the mob is only growing bigger as we plow through traffic and I can't get Girl from Ipanema out of my head. We make it across the High Street bridge with a pack of savage townsfolk on our heals. They're throwing bottles at us as we pass through the midtown wall but they don't follow us through. Still, we're not slowing down for anything. Four more blocks to the city limits, and we're sprinting through the upscale-rent district. Not much foot traffic so we make good time.

Sasha and I are breathing heavy as we meet up with our crew outside of town. Two more are dead. Their bodies have already been looted and the guy who shot Lewis is nowhere to be found. I ask Charles what happened and he tells me they were boxing cacti. From the looks of it they were doing more than that. One of em's got his pants down and he's suspended a good two feet off the ground – impaled on the barbs. The other has a bullet in his head. Clearly the cacti won. Charles insists that it wasn't his idea and he was tricked into coordinating it. Charles then dies from blood loss. He's been bleeding a lot since his arm came off. The Girl from Ipanema is stuck on repeat. The pain. Well, at least we've got gear for the whole crew now.

We wait around a while for Carton to arrive. A pack of Kowbirats have dragged off the corpses and we're watching them feast. The weather is nice. 110° with a warm wind from the west. I hand out gear and everyone suits up. It's like a 3rd grade production of Mad Max – minus the beer. One size fits you, indeed. I do my best to keep the crew from punching cacti, which is more difficult than it sounds. Carton shows up on time and we all pile in. Seating is a bit more even now that our crew has been thinned, so the ride is a comfortable half-hour of much needed rest. The guy who shot Lewis is here too. Not sure how I missed him.

As we head South, I can see the foundation for what will eventually be an irrigation system laid out by the Sluggs. They've been hard at work setting huge pipes to pump water across the planet. Despite all the hostility that Zerth has to offer, there's an equal amount of altruism. It's beautiful. The Sluggs truly are the humanitarians of Zerth. As Carton switches on the radio, I'm finally able to rid my mind of that awful jingle. **Golden Age, by Midnight Oil.** Perfect tune for high speed travel over rocky terrain. Heading due-south at 220mph at an altitude of 700ft. Maybe I should be a pilot. Ships like these aren't too expensive and the Kaggworks is back on it's feet after a 6 year shutdown. They've started incorporating Aerian tech into their new lines and it's got the Morouni in a big kerfuffle, but the prices are dropping and business is booming. I could probably snag a wasp or new pubber for a thousand or so. That'd be a lot of fun. I hear they've got some big project they're keeping secret. Time will tell if it stays that way, but it's keeping the entire town gainfully employed.

We approach the pumpstation and drop in altitude, circling around for a spot to land. I take the opportunity to study the landscape. Rocky with a scattering of hobby trees and a winding inlet at the tail-end of a small range of mountains. The Sluggs deemed the area ideal for a pumpstation and I can see why. It's all even ground with a short drop to the shoreline – maybe 30 feet. We can break ground right there. I jump up from my seat and poke into the cockpit where I'm surprised to find Carton passed out in the corner in a pile of his own offspring. It's like a sleep-orgy. Little Dave is at the helm and he doesn't say a word. I back out of the cockpit and pray for a safe landing.

As we unload from the Often Away, we're surrounded by a welcome party of a hundred happy Sluggs. They're always so damned excited. They offer their services and equipment and even offer to feed us. Nutrient-rich algaecake smoothies – free refills. They don't have mouths so solid food is a no-go. Rather, they soak it all up through their skin. It's not uncommon to find a group of Sluggs 'dining' in their own pot of stew. Thankfully, they've forgone that practice for the moment. As the crew is finishing up their meal, Sasha and I take a moment to look around. Right there, along the ridge would be a perfect spot for a flight tower. I can see it all in my head.

Concerning Flight Towers

I mentioned earlier that I designed these things. The idea was to take an airport and condense the footprint as much as possible. The design was inspired by those plastic Devo hats. Ya know, the one's that look like wedding cakes? I freggin love Devo. Anyway, it's kind of a rounded ziggurat with ten layers. The top is a large concrete dish for loading, as well as the home for the communications kiosk. Up the back side of the tower is the service elevator, which runs from the ground level to the upper dish. It was designed to be a taller structure so ships could embark and disembark above the rooftops of the city.

The interior walls house between 4 to 9 gates for arrivals and departures. UPP-15 ports, to be exact. It's a standard size for cargo ships. The Often Away fits this design perfectly, so you can kind of get an understanding of how the rear of the ship is supposed to pull up and dock with the tower. Unfortunately, what happened is all the gates became magnets for vendors. As flight-masters caught wind of the fact that they could make more money renting out the gates to vendors, passengers instructed their pilots to just drop them off somewhere else rather than be stuck in line waiting for the lunch rush to end.

It's a perfect example of how an idea can be cannibalized. But to be fair, it just goes to show how out of touch I was. It's easy for a guy like me to lose his head in the clouds and become dismantled from reality. When my ideal fantasy clashes with the necessity of others, they blend together, and the degree of frustration is directly proportional to the degree in which my own head was up my ass. The only saving grace is the fact that the idea still remains in my head. So the question is, knowing what I know now, how can I make it work?

As I lose myself to visions of grandeur, I'm drawn back to the loading dish atop the flight tower in Calibur. It was only meant for cargo, but the more I think about it, why couldn't it work for passengers? It was damn near empty up there. All the gates are clogged with vendors anyway, so why fight it? My grand design for a Zertian airport has been devoured by the reality that people would much prefer to be in a shopping mall – and thus, it becomes one. Shopping mall + airport. A place for people to gather and disperse. The only problem is the lack of landing space on the dish. Despite it being empty, if it were to function ideally, it would have to be modified. What if ships didn't land, but rather docked with the dish? You would need some kind of extending platform. Magenite would do it. Yeah, Magenite would also allow for electrical connections to be made; and that way you could keep the craft afloat while it was docked.

Magenite Suspension: A series of 4"x 4"x 120" steel beams equipped with interlocking Magenite clamps, fed through a roller with an electrical contact. When it passes through the roller, the Magenite clamps are introduced to the electrical current and pull together, forming a rigid walkway. The size of the clamps would determine the strength of the walkway, but if it were connected to a power source at both ends, the current would be continuous. It would be as strong as the Magenite itself. I gotta make a phone call.

So, I shoot a message to Amison Kagg, of the Kaggworks. It's a tossup if he actually uses my idea, but I'm hopeful. I ask him to tack on a couple of UPP-1s under all the doorways of his ships to allow for a connection. Not sure if he likes the idea, but he's a Morouni so it's impossible to say one way or another. Either way, I'm satisfied. I take a moment to bask in the glow and pour myself another algaecake smoothie. How sweet it is. The crew is mulling around and waiting for the next shoe to drop. I almost forgot we were supposed to be building something. I put them to work digging a ditch for the irrigation system.   Luckily, we have yet to encounter any Mercs. The crew is decently geared so if it does happen, we will be ready. Sasha is fiddling with his saw-blades and I plop a squat on top of a boulder to keep watch, fidgeting with my new argyle socks.

Concerning Fashion

Much to the dismay of most Humans, everyone seems to dress for the weather. Upon spawning into Zerth and being introduced to a world of flying cars, aliens and plasma rifles, Humans tend to expect more from the attire. Everyone here looks like a bum. And why wouldn't they?

No one cares to waltz around in the 120° heat wearing anything but what is necessary – and what is necessary typically resembles the attire of a transient.

Men's fashion consists of a simple A-shirt, T-shirt or P-shirt made of cotton or linen. If it can breath, it's good enough. Neck-ties and goggles or sunglasses are ubiquitous, as are a good pair of giant boots. Loose fitting pants or bell-bottoms with a holstered pistol is the norm. When traveling, a sturdy overcoat or duster is worn. Women prefer the comfort and simplicity of a sleeveless leotard. Usually accompanied by plunderhose or clam diggers. Like the men, giant boots are imperative, as are goggles or glasses. Longer hair is usually cut or tied up into a bun or ponytail. Holstered pistol is also standard. When traveling, hooded robes are preferred. Generally speaking, the women look no different from the men. Unisex is key, as many of the beings of Zerth are sexless Legomi and Sluggs.

Humans introduced baseball caps, which are usually worn backwards, keeping the suns off the back of the neck. Sunglasses or shaded goggles are a must. No one wants to walk around blind, except the Legomi, who find the practice of blinding ones self quite hilarious.

Neck-ties are a necessity. Not only do they fashionably bisect one's form vertically, but they're also handy in a bind, or *to* bind. For their multi-purpose wonder, neck-ties are generally much more durable than their Earthly counterparts, and are often worn without a shirt. Boots are a must. No one goes anywhere without their boots. Some travel with a spare set around their neck as the rough terrain has a tendency to eat them. They are usually made from macromite hide. The beast's rock-like skin offers perfect protection for the weary travelers feet, and can be boiled and eaten if one were so inclined.

Tattoos are everywhere, though piercings are not. Sectoids were marked at birth when the Aerie Empire was big news, but since then, the standard downward arrow design has become a bit taboo. No one faults a Sectoid for sporting the head-mark, as it had only been a few years since the fall, but newer offspring have been allowed the choice in what to smear across their foreheads. Legomi skin doesn't take ink well, so all tattoos were temporary to them, but Sectoids and Humans ink themselves up like drunken sailors, eager to plaster their personalities across their skin. Piercings are another matter altogether. Legomi skin swallows them and Slugg skin is too tough to pierce. Morouni and Humans are the only ones to take up the fashion, as Sectoids mocked the practice of poking holes just to fill them up with dirty jewelry. Piercing is left to the overly-hygienic, as the sand truly gets everywhere.

Tobacco is highly fashionable among men, women and genderless alike. Any smoker inevitably devotes half their garden towards tobacco, as it's so easy and quick to grow in the home. Many flavors are added, including winegrass (similar to grape in flavor) knuckeberry (slight taste of Anise) and bourbon. Osha root is also smoked quite commonly, as the species is native to the Zerth. Turmeric as well, though smoking turmeric tends to turn one's teeth yellow (and in the case of the Legomi, turn their skin bright red.)

Cigars and cigarettes are self rolled and pipes carved from—oh wow. **Who Cares Why – The Brian Jonestown Massacre**. This is some heady music. My compliments to the DJ. The suns are setting and the beat is—oh shit, the guy who shot Lewis is running over the workers! He's in the steam-roller and he's driving through the ditch! "That's not what the steam-roller is for", I yell, but he isn't responding. They aren't even moving out of the way. Are they suicidal? I turn to Sasha but it's no use. He's died of the Sniffles. Dead in the dirt, mid-sneeze.

Jesus Christ. I take off towards the crew, shouting, but it's too late – they're all gone. The guy who shot Lewis hops off the steamroller and apologizes for passing out at the wheel. He's smiling. A mess of Sluggs crowd around the linear gore, weeping and falling on their knees. The guy who shot Lewis assures them that nothing is out of the ordinary and that the workers will be fine, to which the Sluggs cheer and applaud his fortitude. They're shaking his hand and congratulating him. He tells me to calm down, and that I'm just having a bad case of the Onesdays. I want to punch him in the mouth. What a goddamned mess. 28 workers lost, several hundred bucks down the drain and now I've got to stop what I'm doing to go get Sasha.

So, I'm back in the Often Away with the guy who shot Lewis. I'll give him credit, he is charismatic. He does his best to keep my spirits up as we race across the Burning Basin, en route to Azura. Its a sour return. Everything up to this point has been wasted. Or has it? I suppose without all these shenanigans, I may never have come up with the idea for Magenite Suspension. Good ideas are funny that way. So much goes into them that it's impossible to find their source. You can point to one thing or another; but, inevitably it's the result of a chain of events that were significant enough to stick in your brain and mix with the things you know to be true. If it jives, it comes out the other end as something amazing. I'm not going to get ahead of myself. I'm not even sure if it will work, but the science is sound. We will see. **The Bomb by The Bucketheads** intrudes upon my mind and I'm just not having it. The guy who shot Lewis can't get enough. Good for him. He's not the greatest dancer, but that isn't stopping him. I wish someone would stop the DJ. The beat drowns out the sunlight, giving The Girl from Ipanema a run for its money as the low point of my day.

As we head Eastward through Anu Bardus, the gleam of Aerie Tower pierces the windows and fills the guy who shot Lewis's eyes with stars. A big shining finger in the sand – about 30 miles off the port side. He wants to know what it is. I tell him it's the remains of the Aerie Empire, and that there are still some Aerie loyalists who live there. He says he wants to blow it up. A lot of people say that. What is it about free-standing structures in conspicuous locations that just beg to be torn down? Its like an innate sense of order – we see something that doesn't belong and we want to wreck it. I'll admit, the idea is pretty enticing. The guy who shot Lewis is making plans as we approach our destination.

Azura. I have memories of this place. I'm not going to say fond memories, nor will I say they are all that bad. Maybe a bit too familiar in all the wrong ways. The waiting room of the hospital; that's what Azura is to me. It's got a different feel than I remember from so many years ago. The wonder is gone, replaced by a blunt familiarity. The great wall is still here, as is the creek. The ruins still stand, but now prop up advertisements and banners. The fishers are having a beer under a bright red tarp and chatting about spending money. Someone's got balloons up around the shattered courtyard and there's a sign with the words "Beagle's Deagles: Kill Me!" There's a pile of corpses off to the side, presumably Beagle's. The guy who shot Lewis is intrigued and wanders off to scrounge.

The DJ's got speakers up here too, greeting the traveler's return to the tune of **Soundgarden's Never the Machine Forever.** Jesus Christ. If there were ever a way to really upset someone, this would be it. What do you tell someone facing this kind of nonsense? No, ma'am, you aren't dead, though it is possible you are in hell – that's still up for debate. Yes, that *is* one of those gray aliens you saw in Fire in the Sky. Yes, that *is* a talking sprig of broccoli, and yes, you are listening to Soundgarden. No, you aren't dreaming, and no, I won't drive you to your daughter's house. She can't help you here. Can I get you a drink? Pretty rough.

I hear Sasha's voice from beyond the rubble. He's soaked, pulling himself out of the creek and laughing. "Just a little swim in river," he says with a smile, "and look, no more sniffles!" He's in a great mood. The fishers rush to his aid, waving papers in his face, but I call them off, assuring them that he's a respawn. Sasha asks about the crew and I tell him we're heading back to Ghong for more. No need to go into the ugly details. I ask him how Earth is doing in 1983. He says he still prefers vodka over his wife.

We linger, gabbing about Earth and all its trouble. As we talk, I notice something under my foot. I kick at the sand and uncover something I didn't expect to find. A memory. A little plastic bottle labeled "Deths-Head Moonshine". It belonged to Walt. I chuckle to myself. How strange things were back then – taking turns shooting Walt in the face; then he would take over and do it himself. I remember the look of terror in his eyes when we first decided to do it. Genuine fear – and what else would it be? But after a while, that fear faded and he really took control. I remember the last thing he said to me. "After gettin' shot in the face 100 times, divorce ain't even an issue." He had that look in his eyes like he found something beautiful. Like the tangled mess inside his head was finally unwound and straightened out. I still remember the way he laughed, like he didn't care about the world anymore. He laughed like he knew it was all his fault and finally figured out how to fix it. He didn't show up after that, and you know what? I don't think he minds at all.

About the Author

Mighty Rahiem is a deep-state agent; a CIA stooge.
He enjoys hiking, fly fishing and destabilizing fictitious
countries with his cyclotron.

More from Mighty Rahiem

and Zerthbooks.com

Available Now!

At Amazon.com and

Zerthbooks.com